ISBN 1-84135-191-1

Copyright © 2003 Award Publications Limited

First published 2003

Published by Award Publications Limited,
27 Longford Street, London NW1 3DZ

Printed in Malaysia

Award Young Readers

Goldilocks and the Three Bears

Rewritten by Jackie Andrews
Illustrated by Lawrie Taylor

AWARD PUBLICATIONS LIMITED

Once upon a time there were three bears who lived in a cottage deep in the heart of a wood. There was a great, big father bear, a middle-sized mother bear, and a tiny weeny baby bear.

Every morning they cooked porridge for their breakfast, and every morning they all went out for a walk in the wood while their porridge cooled.

One day, while the three bears were out enjoying their morning walk, a little girl called Goldilocks was also out in the wood.

She had been picking flowers and had wandered rather a long way from home.

"Oh dear," she said. "I hope I find a house soon. I think I'm lost. I shall have to ask someone the way home."

And then she saw the cottage where the bears lived.

Goldilocks knocked on the cottage door.
There was no reply.

"Oh, there's no one at home," she said,
disappointed. Then she turned the handle and
found that the door wasn't locked.

"But I'm sure they won't mind if I go in and
wait for them."

And that's just what she did.

Goldilocks stepped into the kitchen and looked round. It was all very neat and tidy and there was a wonderful smell of porridge in the air. It made her feel very hungry.

She went over to the table and saw the three bowls of porridge: a great big bowl, a middle-sized bowl and a tiny weeny bowl.

"It won't hurt to have just a little taste," she said.

And she pulled out the biggest chair.

It was Father Bear's great big chair.

Goldilocks sat down and tried the porridge in the great big bowl.

"Ow, ow!" she cried, dropping the spoon. "This porridge is far too hot!"

She went to Mother Bear's middle-sized chair and tried the porridge in the middle-sized bowl.

"Ugh!" she said. "This porridge is much too cold!"

There was one bowl left. Goldilocks sat down in Baby Bear's tiny weeny chair and tried the porridge in the tiny weeny bowl.

"Mmmm," she said, licking her lips. "This porridge is just right!"

And she ate thc lot.

Goldilocks began to feel sleepy. She went into the next room and saw three comfy chairs.

"I'm sure no one will mind if I have a little rest," she said.

She went over and sat in Father Bear's great big armchair.

"Ow, ow!" she cried. "This chair is much too hard."

She went over and sat in Mother Bear's middle-sized armchair.

"Oh, no!" she sighed, as she sank into the cushions. "This chair is much too soft."

There was one tiny weeny chair left. "This looks just right," said Goldilocks.

And she sat down in Baby Bear's chair.

Unfortunately, Goldilocks was rather heavy for
the tiny weeny chair. It broke, and Goldilocks
tumbled to the floor.
She got up crossly and
stamped up the stairs
to the bedroom.

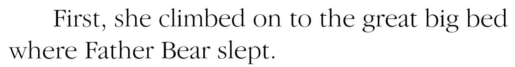

First, she climbed on to the great big bed
where Father Bear slept.

"Ow, ow!" she cried. "This bed is much
too hard."

Then she tried the middle-sized bed where Mother Bear slept.

"Oh no," she sighed as she sank into the mattress. "This bed is much too soft."

There was one tiny weeny bed left. "This looks just right," said Goldilocks, and she got into Baby Bear's bed and fell fast asleep.

Now while Goldilocks was sleeping, the three bears came home from their walk. They were looking forward to their breakfast and took their places at the table.

"Look at that!" said Father Bear, in his great big growly voice. "Somebody's been eating my porridge!"

"Oh my goodness," said Mother Bear in her soft, middle-sized voice. "Somebody's been eating my porridge, too!"

"Oh no!" squeaked Baby Bear in his tiny weeny voice. "Somebody's been eating my porridge – and it's all gone!"

And it was then that Father Bear noticed their favourite chairs.

"Look at that!" said Father Bear, in his great big growly voice. "Somebody's been sitting in my chair!"

"And look!" said Mother Bear in her soft, middle-sized voice. "Somebody's been sitting in my chair, too!"

"Oh no!" cried Baby Bear in his tiny weeny voice. "Somebody's been sitting in my chair – and it's all broken!"

The three bears decided to look upstairs in the bedroom.

Up the stairs they climbed. And all this time,
Goldilocks was still fast asleep.

"Look at that!" said Father Bear, in his great
big growly voice. "Somebody's been sleeping in
my bed!"

"My goodness!" said Mother Bear in her soft,
middle-sized voice. "Somebody's been sleeping in
my bed, too!"

"Oh no!" cried Baby Bear in his tiny weeny voice. "Somebody's been sleeping in my bed – AND SHE'S STILL HERE!"

The three bears all stood round Baby Bear's bed, staring – in amazement – at Goldilocks.

Goldilocks woke up with a start. Unable to believe her eyes, she saw three furry bear faces looking down at her.

"Oh! Oh!" she shrieked.

She tossed back the covers and
leaped out of bed, ran down the stairs, and
out of the back door as fast as she could. And the
three bears were too surprised to say anything.

It was, of course, the last they ever saw of
Goldilocks.